Hurray for Barbara Park
and the Junie B. Jones® books!

Check out Barbara Park's other great books, listed at the end of this book!

Junie B. Jones®
and That
Meanie Jim's Birthday

BY BARBARA PARK

illustrated by
Denise Brunkus

A STEPPING STONE BOOK™

Random House 🏠 New York

Copyright © 1996 by Barbara Park
Illustrations copyright © 1996 by Denise Brunkus

All rights reserved. Published in the United States by Random House Children's Books, a division of Random House, Inc., New York.

RANDOM HOUSE and colophon are registered trademarks and A STEPPING STONE BOOK and colophon are trademarks of Random House, Inc. JUNIE B. JONES is a registered trademark of Barbara Park, used under license.

www.randomhouse.com/kids/junieb

Educators and librarians, for a variety of teaching tools, visit us at www.randomhouse.com/teachers

Library of Congress Cataloging-in-Publication Data
Park, Barbara.
Junie B. Jones and that meanie Jim's birthday / by Barbara Park ; illustrated by Denise Brunkus.
    p.   cm. "A stepping stone book."
SUMMARY: Junie B. is very upset when a boy in her class plans to invite everyone except her to his birthday party, but her grandfather helps her deal with the situation.
ISBN 978-0-679-86695-4 (pbk.) — ISBN 978-0-679-96695-1 (lib. bdg.)
[1. Kindergarten—Fiction.   2. Schools—Fiction.   3. Behavior—Fiction.
4. Grandfathers—Fiction.]   I. Brunkus, Denise, ill.   II. Title.
PZ7.P2197Jtsl   1996   [Fic]—dc20   95-35513

Printed in the United States of America   55 54 53 52 51 50 49 48 47

Contents

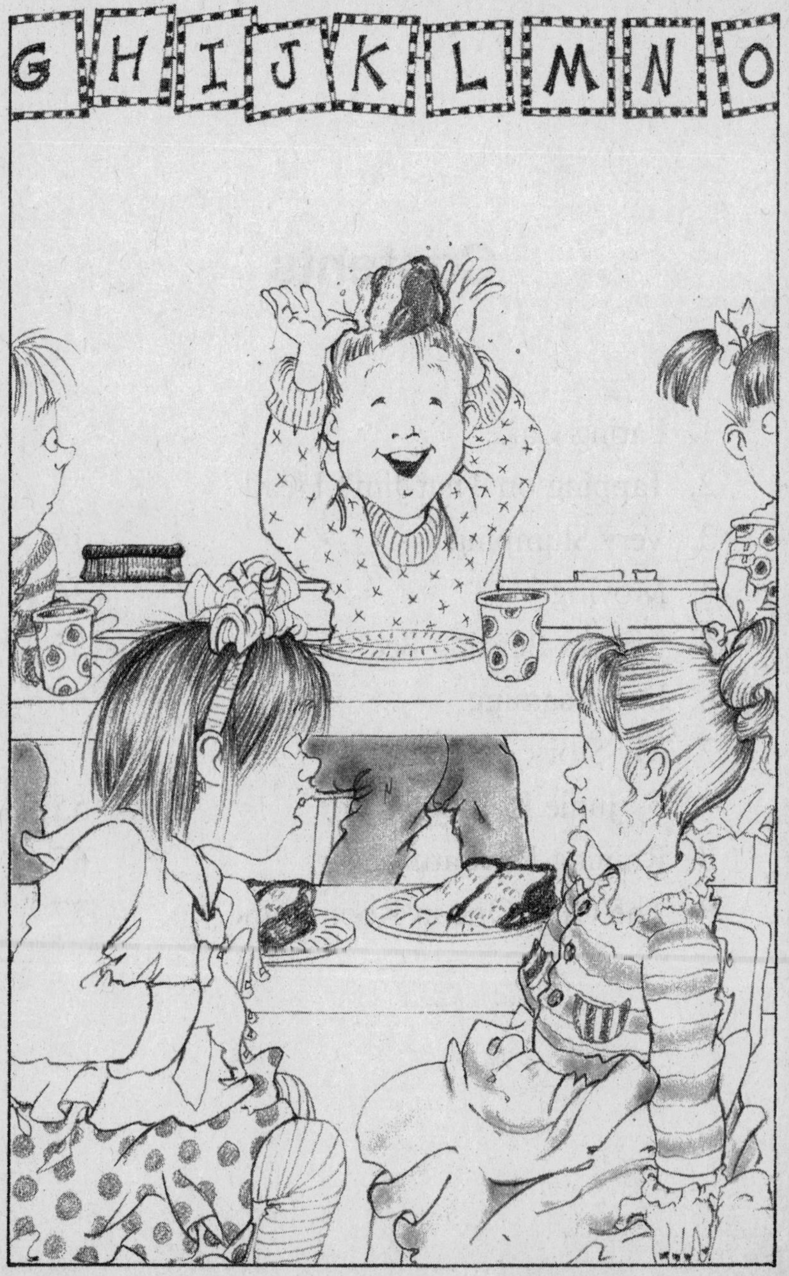
G H I J K L M N O

1/
Eating Cake

My name is Junie B. Jones. The B stands for Beatrice. Except I don't like Beatrice. I just like B and that's all.

B is my bestest letter. On account of my favorite food starts with that guy.

Its name is birthday cake.

We had that delicious stuff at school today.

That's because Paulie Allen Puffer turned six years old. And his mother brought chocolate cake and chocolate ice cream and chocolate milk to Room Nine.

She is a chocolate nut, I think.

The party was very fun.

Except for Paulie Allen Puffer got all wound up. And he put cake on his head. And then he laughed till milk came out his nose.

"That is called nose milk," I told my bestest friend named Lucille.

Lucille is a little lady.

"Eew," she said. "I wish I didn't even see that nose milk. 'Cause now my stomach feels upset. And I can't eat the rest of my cake."

"Me too," I said. "Now I can't eat the rest of my cake, too. And so I will throw both our cakes in the trash can for us."

Then I picked up our cakes. And I hurried up to the trash can.

I looked all around me very careful.

Then I quick ducked behind the trash can.

And I stuffed both those cakes right in my mouth.

I rubbed my tummy real happy.

"Now all I need is some milk to wash it down with," I said.

That's when I saw some milk sitting on a table. All by itself.

I picked it up. And drank it all gone.

"Mmmm," I said. "That hit the spot!"

Just then, I heard a voice.

"Junie B. Jones? Why are you out of your seat?"

It was my teacher.

Her name is Mrs.

She has another name, too. But I just like Mrs. and that's all.

Mrs. has eyes like a hawk.

"What are you doing over there?" she asked me.

"I am sharing people's cake and milk," I explained. "Except for they aren't actually here at the moment."

Mrs. rolled her eyes way back in her head.

I smiled very sweet.

"Guess what? When I have *my* birthday party, I am going to bring cake and milk, too," I said. "Plus also, I might bring a beanie weenie casserole. 'Cause that will be a nice change of pace, I think."

Just then, I skipped over to Paulie Allen Puffer's mother.

"Excellent cake, madam. My compliments to the *chief*," I said.

Then me and her did a high-five. Only she didn't actually put her hand out. And so mostly I just slapped her on the arm.

After that, I skipped back to my seat.

Lucille was finishing her chocolate ice cream.

She had a chocolate mustache on her lip.

I did a frown at her.

"Lucille, I am surprised at you," I said. "You are not eating that ice cream like a little lady. And so I will show you how."

Then I quick dipped my spoon into Lucille's ice cream.

"See?" I said. "See how I am taking dainty bites of this stuff?"

Only just then, a dainty bite of chocolate ice cream slipped off my spoon. And it plopped into Lucille's lap.

She jumped out of her chair.

"OH NO!" she hollered. "NOW LOOK WHAT YOU DID! YOU SPILLED ICE

CREAM ON MY BRAND-NEW DRESS! AND MY NANNA JUST BROUGHT THIS TO ME FROM NEW YORK CITY! AND IT COSTED NINETY-FIVE DOLLARS PLUS TAX!"

Mrs. hurried up to my table. She had a wet sponge to clean Lucille's dress.

"No! Don't!" said Lucille. "You can't put water on this! 'Cause this dress is made of satin! And satin is dry clean only!"

Mrs. made angry eyes at me.

I did a gulp.

"Who knew?" I said real soft.

Then I put my head down on my table.

And I covered up with my arms.

'Cause that is called laying low.

And laying low is what you do if you know what's good for you.

2/
Tapping on
That Jim's Head

After the party, me and my other bestest friend rode home on the bus.

Her name is Grace.

Me and that Grace take turns sitting next to the window.

That is good sports of us, I think.

Except for sometimes we forget whose turn it is.

Then we have to settle it with our fists.

This time, it was that Grace's turn to sit

next to the window.

"Guess what? I don't even care if you sit there today," I told her. "'Cause eating all that cake made me in a happy mood."

That Grace smiled.

"Me too," she said. "Eating that cake made me in a happy mood, too."

"Yeah, only you can't be as happy as me," I explained. "'Cause I had two cakes. And you just had one."

That Grace did a frown.

"That's okay, Grace. Don't be upset," I said. "'Cause when I have my birthday, I will invite you to my house. And you can have two cakes, too."

"Oh boy!" she said.

"I know it is *oh boy*," I said back. "Plus also, you will get your very own paper cup with M&M's in it."

"Ooooh! Yum! I *love* M&M's," said that Grace.

"Me too. I love M&M's, too," I said. "On account of the chocolate doesn't melt on your hands. Just the colors melt on your hands and that's all."

I smiled real big.

"And here's *another* good thing, Grace. When you come to my party, you will get your very own party hat. And we will play Twister. Plus also, we will play that game where you shout Bingo. Only I keep on forgetting the name of that one."

Just then, a meanie boy named Jim jumped up from his seat.

"BINGO, stupid!" he shouted. "Its name is BINGO! What a MORON! Who would even want to come to a stupid party like yours?"

He made his voice real loud. So everybody could hear.

"At *my* house I have *cool* birthday parties," he said. "Like last year my party was named Clowning Around. And we had two clowns from the circus. And they made balloon animals and did magic tricks."

I leaned way close to his face.

"So?" I said. "I don't even *like* clowns. Clowns are not normal people. Plus my very own grampa Frank Miller can make balloon animals, too. Except for they all look like wiener dogs. Only he's working on it."

That Jim wasn't even listening to me. He just kept on talking about his parties.

"*This* year my party is named Old MacDonald's Farm. And a real farmer is bringing a petting zoo right to my front yard. And he's going to bring a lamb, and a goat, and a burro, and some rabbits! And he's also bringing a real, live pony for us to ride!"

I put my hands on my waist.

"Yeah, well, too bad for you," I said. "'Cause I saw all about ponies on TV. And

ponies buck you off their backs. And then they stomple you into the ground and kill you to death. And so I wouldn't even come to your stupid dumb party in a jillion billion years."

"Good!" hollered that Jim. "I'm glad! 'Cause my birthday is this coming Saturday! And tomorrow I'm bringing invitations to every single person in Room Nine! Only *not* to you! You're the *only one* in the whole class I'm not bringing an invitation to! So there!"

Then he did a big HAH! right in my face.

And he sat back down in his seat.

Meanwhile, I just kept on standing and standing there.

'Cause something had gone a little bit wrong here, I think.

I tapped on his head.

"Yeah, only here's the thing," I said. "I didn't actually know you were having a party on Saturday. And so, good news . . . I think I can make it."

"No!" shouted that meanie boy. "You're not coming! Now go away!"

I tapped on him again.

"Yeah, only I was just kidding about the ponies," I said. "They hardly even stomple you, probably."

"I don't care! Stop bothering me!" he shouted.

I stood on my tippy-toes and looked at his head.

"Love your hair today," I said.

That Jim swatted at me.

"Get away from me!" he hollered. "You're not coming to my party! And that's final!"

Just then, a big lump came in my throat. A big lump is what comes before crying.

It hurt to swallow.

I sat down and hided my face in my sweater.

"Darn it," I said. "'Cause I think I really would have enjoyed myself at that thing."

Then my bestest friend named Grace put her arm around me.

And she patted me real gentle.

And she let me sit next to the window.

3/
Very Slumping

I walked home from the bus stop very slumping.

Very slumping is when your shoulders are sad. And your head can't hold up that good.

Grandma Miller was in the nursery.

She baby-sits me and my baby brother in the afternoon.

His name is Ollie.

I love him a real lot. Except I wish he didn't live at my actual house.

Grandma Miller was rocking him in the rocking chair.

I tried to climb up there, too. Only Grandma said "Hold your horses" at me.

"Yeah, only I need to rock very bad," I explained. "On account of a mean boy is having a birthday party on Saturday. And he is inviting everyone in Room Nine. Only not me. I'm the *only one* who's not going."

Grandma Miller did a sad face.

"Children can be so cruel," she said. "Just wait till I get the baby to sleep. And then you and I will talk about it. Okay?"

And so that's how come I crossed my arms.

And I tapped my foot.

And I waited and waited for that baby to go to sleep. Only his eyes kept on staying wide open.

"Hold them closed with your fingers, Grandma," I told her.

"Heavens, no!" she said.

Then she kept right on rocking him.

And so finally I got tired of waiting. And I went to my room. And I crawled underneath my covers.

I crawled way down to the bottom of my sheets.

It is very muffly down there.

You can say mean stuff.

And no one can hear you.

"Here is all the stuff I hate," I said. "First, I hate that meanie Jim. Then I hate

clowns. And Old MacDonald had a farmer. Plus I hate rabbits. And burros. And ponies.

"And guess what else? We didn't actually need a baby at this house. Only no one even consulted me."

Just then, I heard a knock on my door.

"Junie B.? It's Grandma, honey. Ollie finally went to sleep."

She came in and lifted up my covers.

"I called your mother and told her what happened at school," she said.

I peeked up at her.

"And so can she fix it?" I asked. "Can I go to the birthday party now?"

Grandma Miller held out her arms to me.

She pulled me out of my covers.

"Your mother is going to talk to you about it when she gets home," she said.

"Meanwhile, why don't you and I have a little fun. Let's read a book, okay? What kind of story would you like to hear?"

I thought and thought.

"I would like to hear a story about a little girl who doesn't get invited to a meanie boy's birthday. And so she sneaks to his house. And she lets a wild pony out of the barn. And then it stomples the boy into a flattie pancake. And all the children pour maple syrup on that guy. And they eat him for breakfast."

Grandma Miller looked kind of sickish.

"You've got to stop worrying about that boy's party. He's just trying to get your goat," she said.

Just then, my eyes got big and wide at her.

"Goat? What goat, Grandma? Do I have

a goat? Is it a surprise goat? Are you keep-
ing it a secret at your house?"

I jumped up and pulled her hand.

"Let's go get it! Want to, Grandma?
Let's go get my goat right now!"

Just then, a great idea popped in my head.

"HEY! I JUST THOUGHT OF SOME-
THING, GRANDMA! YOU AND ME
CAN BRING MY GOAT TO MY HOUSE!
AND THEN I CAN HAVE MY VERY
OWN BIRTHDAY ON SATURDAY!

"I WILL CALL IT 'COME AND PET
MY GOAT'! AND EVERYONE IN
ROOM NINE WILL COME TO MY
PARTY! AND THEY WON'T GO TO
THAT MEANIE JIM'S!"

All of a sudden, the front door opened.

It was Mother!

I runned to her speedy quick.

"Mother! Mother! Guess what? Guess what? Me and Grandma Miller are getting my goat! And I am having my very own birthday party on Saturday! And all of Room Nine is going to be invited. Only not that Jim I hate! He is the *only one* not coming! So ha ha on him!"

Just then, Grandma Miller sneaked out the front door with her sweater.

I pulled on Mother's arm.

"Come on, Mother! Come on!" I said. "We have to go to the store and buy my invitations! Plus also, we have to pick up the beanie weenies!"

Mother didn't come on.

She sat down on the couch. And smoothed my hair.

"Listen to me, Junie B.," she said. "I know Jim hurt your feelings today. But you can't have your birthday party on Saturday. Your birthday isn't till June, remember? And June is still months away."

"I know June is months away," I said. "And so that is how come I am moving my birthday sooner. 'Cause months away will be too late."

Mother picked me up and put me on her lap.

"I'm afraid you don't understand, honey," she said. "You just can't *change* the day you were born. No one can. It's impossible."

I made my voice very whispering.

"Yeah, only here's a little secret . . . nobody in Room Nine even knows when my birthday is. So I think we can pull it off."

Mother did a little smile. She ruffled my hair.

"Sorry, honey. No can do," she said.

"Yes!" I hollered. "Yes can do! 'Cause I *have* to have my birthday on Saturday! Or else I will be the *only one* who is not going to that meanie Jim's! And that is the saddest story I ever even heard of."

Just then, my eyes got a little bit of wet in them.

Mother wiped my face with a tissue.

Then she hugged me real tight.

And she said the words *I'm sorry.*

More bad news.

Grandma Miller just called . . .

There's no goat.

4/ Moving

The next morning, I didn't get out of my bed.

Not even when Mother hollered, "Time for breakfast."

She came into my room.

"Didn't you hear me, Junie B.? It's time to eat," she said.

I looked up from my pillow.

"Yeah, only I'm not even hungry. Plus also, I'm moving today," I said.

Mother smiled.

She sat on my bed.

"You're moving, huh?" she asked. "And exactly where will you be going?"

I did my shoulders up and down.

"Somewhere," I said.

"Somewhere, where?" she asked.

"Somewhere not here, that's where," I said.

Mother hugged me.

"This is still about Jim's birthday party, isn't it?" she said. "You're still worried about not getting an invitation."

"No, I'm not," I said. "On account of I'm not even going to that school anymore. On account of I'm moving today."

Mother shook her head. Then she went out of my room. And she and Daddy did whispering in the hall.

Pretty soon, Daddy came in.

He gave me a piggyback ride to the
kitchen.

Then Mother made my favorite hot
cereal.

And she let me have all the brown sugar
I wanted.

She sat down next to me.

"You know, Junie B., Jim is only doing this to hurt your feelings," she said. "He just wants to get a reaction from you, that's all."

"Sure, he does," said Daddy. "And when someone is trying to hurt your feelings, there's only one way to get back at them."

"You have to pretend you don't care," said Mother. "You have to pretend you don't even *want* to go to that party. Because if you pretend you don't want to go, it will take all the fun out of it for him."

Daddy winked.

"You can do that, can't you?" he asked. "You're the best little pretender in the entire *world*."

Just then, my whole face lighted up. 'Cause that word gave me a great idea!

"Hey! I just figured out where I can move to! It's called It's a Small World After

29

All. And it's at Disneyland! 'Member that, Daddy? It's where all those puppets keep on singing that same song over and over and over again."

I smiled. "That would be a happy place to live, don't you think?"

Daddy looked at me a real long time.

Then he put his head down on the table. And he started knocking it on the edge.

Mother pulled him up from there.

They went in the hall and did more whispering.

After a while, Mother called to me from her bedroom.

"Junie B.? Could you pick up the phone, please? It's your grandfather. He wants to talk to you for a minute."

I picked up the phone. "H'lo?"

"Hello yourself, little girl," said my

grampa Frank Miller. "What'cha up to this morning?"

"I'm moving today," I told him.

Grampa Miller sounded upset.

"Moving?" he said. "Oh no! You *can't* be moving! If you move, then you won't be able to come over to my house on Saturday!"

I crinkled up my eyebrows at him.

'Cause this conversation smelled fishy, that's why.

"Yeah, only how come you want me to come to your house?" I asked. "And how come it has to be on Saturday?"

"Because Saturday's the day I do my work around here, remember?" he said. "You're still my little helper, aren't you?"

I thought very careful.

"Yes," I said.

31

On account of sometimes I help Grampa fix stuff. It is called odd jobs, I think.

"Are you doin' odd jobs?" I asked him. "Is that why you want me to come there?"

"Sure I'm doin' odd jobs," said my grampa. "But I can't do them without my helper, can I? You're the one who wears the tool belt, aren't you?"

I smiled very proud. 'Cause Grampa Miller's tool belt is the bestest thing I love. It has a jillion tools hanging off of that thing. It wraps around me two whole times. And I don't even cave in.

Just then, Grampa Miller made his voice real quiet.

"You haven't even heard the best part yet," he whispered. "Guess what I'm going to be fixing?"

I whispered back at him. "What?"

Then Grampa said for me to hang on a minute. On account of he wanted to close his door. Or else my grandma might hear.

"If your grandma hears, then *she'll* want to be my helper, instead of you," he said.

I waited very patient.

"Ready?" he said.

"Ready," I said.

"Okay. I'm going to be fixing the upstairs *toilet*."

Just then, my mouth came all the way open.

'Cause fixing the upstairs toilet is a dream come true, that's why!

"Are you gonna take the lid off the top, Grampa? And are you gonna keep flushing it and flushing it? And are you gonna watch all the water go out of that thing?" I asked.

"Sure I am! Of course I am! That's half

the fun of fixing the toilet! Right?" he said.

"Right!" I said very excited. "Plus also, I love that big ball that floats on the top."

"Me too!" said my grampa. "I love that big ball, too! And so I can count on you, can't I? You and I have a date on Saturday, right?"

I thought some more.

"Yeah, only I think there's something you forgot, Grampa."

"What?" he asked. "What did I forget, little girl?"

I raised my eyebrows at that sillyhead.

"You forgot that I'm moving today."

5/
Being a Buzzing Bee

Grandma and Grampa Miller take turns baby-sitting me before lunch. Then they get me dressed for kindergarten.

Except for today, Mother came home from work. And she got me dressed instead.

She said she would drive me to school.

"If I drive you, then you won't have to see Jim on the bus," she said very thoughtful.

She got out my clothes for school.

It was my jumper with the frogs on it.

"Yeah, only guess what? I'm not even wearing school clothes today. On account of I'm moving. And so I have to wear moving man clothes."

Mother kept on trying to put that jumper on me.

That's how come I made my legs and arms real stiff. So they wouldn't fit in there that good.

Then me and Mother wrestled a teeny bit. And she stood me on my head. And she pulled my tights on me.

"You're not moving, Junie B.," she said. "You're going to school, and that's final. Running away from your problems never solves anything."

"Yeah, only I'm not even running," I said. "I'm calling Ryder Rents Trucks. And those guys will drive me."

Mother smiled. She tried to hug me. But I kept on staying real stiff.

I stayed real stiff all the way in the car to school.

Mother parked the car in the parking lot.

Then she lifted me out the door. And she carried me real stiff to the playground.

She stood me up in the grass.

"Everything will be fine. You'll see," she said. "Just remember what Daddy and I told you. If anyone talks about the party, pretend it doesn't bother you."

She kissed me goodbye on my stiff head.

Just then, I heard voices hollering.

"JUNIE B.! HEY, JUNIE B.! LOOK! LOOK WHAT WE GOT!" they hollered.

I turned around.

It was my bestest friends, Lucille and that Grace. They were running at me.

"Look!" said Lucille. "Look what Jim gave us! It's invitations to his birthday party on Saturday!"

"It's just like he told us, Junie B.!" said that Grace. "He's really gonna have a petting zoo there!"

I quick covered my ears with my hands.

Then I closed my eyes. And I sang a loud song at them.

It is called "I Can't Hear You, You're Not Even Botherin' Me."

I sang it at the top of my lungs.

"I CAAA-ANNN'T HEARRRR YOU!

"I CAAA-ANNN'T HEARRRR YOU!

"YOU'RE NOT E-VEN BOTHERIN' MEEEE!"

Then I kept on singing and singing that thing till they went away.

Also, they did the cuckoo sign at me.

After that, I sat down in the grass all by myself. And I looked all around the playground.

Lots of other children had invitations, too.

"Darn it," I whispered. "Darn it. Darn it. Darn it."

That's when I saw that meanie Jim.

He was giving an invitation to a boy named Crybaby William.

Crybaby William is the scarediest cat in Room Nine.

He is even scared of a teeny flea, I think.

Just then, I sat up a little bit straighter.

'Cause I just got another idea in my head, that's why!

It was called, Hey! Maybe I can take William's invitation away from him! 'Cause he won't even chase me, probably! And so then I will have my very own invitation! And William can get another one from that Jim! And then *everybody* will get to go to the party. Including me!

I stood up from the grass.

Then I squinted my eyes at Crybaby William. And I started to run at him very slow.

I runned faster and faster. Till finally, I was running as fast as a speeding bumble-bee.

I buzzed all around William zippity quick.

His eyes couldn't even follow me that good.

Then I buzzed right in his face. And I quick grabbed that invitation out of his fingers!

I runned my fastest to the swing set!

And guess what?

William didn't even follow me! That's what!

And here's more good news! William's invitation didn't even have his name on it! So that means it can be for *anybody*, probably!

"Only now it's mine!" I said. "'Cause I will put my name on it when I get to Room Nine! And it will be my very own invitation!"

Just then, the bell rang for school.

I put my invitation way down in my

deep pocket. And I skipped very happy to my class.

Mrs. was standing outside of Room Nine.

William was standing with her.

His nose was sniffling a real lot.

I tried to skip past them. But Mrs. grabbed the straps of my frog jumper.

She pulled me back.

"Yeah, only I don't actually think that is good for the outfit," I said.

Mrs. did a frown.

"Junie B., did you take something that belonged to William?" she asked.

"No," I said. "'Cause his name wasn't even on it. And so that means it is for anybody, I think."

Mrs. tapped her angry foot.

"Was William *holding* an invitation,

Junie B.? And did you snatch it out of his hands? And then did you run away from him?" she asked.

I smiled very cute.

"I was a buzzing bee," I said.

Mrs. holded out her hand.

"May I have it, please?" she asked. "May I have the invitation you took from William?"

I rocked back and forth on my feet.

'Cause I didn't want to give it to her, that's why.

"Yeah, only I think it mighta bounced out of my pocket," I said.

Mrs. bended down next to me. She leaned way into my face.

"I want that invitation," she said. "*Now.*"

I did a gulp.

Then I quick put my hand in my pocket.

"Good news. I found it," I said very nervous.

"Give it to William," said Mrs.

Crybaby William put out his hand.

I shoved it at him.

"Here, Mr. Stinkyhead Tattletale Boy," I said. "Here's your stinkyhead invitation."

Mrs.'s eyes got real big.

"Junie B. Jones! That's quite enough! Now you go sit down! And I don't want to hear another word. Do you understand, young lady? Not one more word."

And so that's how come I walked very slumping to my seat.

And I put my head on my table.

'Cause guess why?

Laying low again, that's why.

6/
Daydreaming

Mrs. took attendance. Attendance is when you say, *I'm here*. Except if you're not here, you have to be quiet.

Also, we said, *I pledge allegiance to the flag of the United States of America.*

That is called opening ceremonies, I think.

After that, we sat down. And Mrs. passed out our workbooks.

She told us the pages to turn to.

It was work about different kinds of

shapes. Like circles. And squares. And tri-ankles.

I am a breeze at that stuff.

Only I couldn't even concentrate very good. On account of I kept daydreaming about that birthday party.

Daydreaming is just like night dreaming.

Only it's not night.

And you're not asleep.

And you're not dreaming.

I kept on thinking about how everybody was going to that party.

Only not me.

I was the *only one*.

In *all* of Room Nine.

I wish Lucille and Grace weren't going, too, I thought to just myself. *'Cause that would be nice sports of them.*

After a while, I tapped on Lucille.

"You are my bestest good friend," I told her.

Lucille smiled at me.

"You are my bestest good friend, too," she said.

I touched her new dress.

"You look very precious today," I said.

Lucille fluffed herself.

"Thank you. You look very precious today, too," she said back.

I touched her fingernails with polish on them.

"I wish you and me could be twins," I said.

"Me too. I wish you and me could be twins, too," she said.

Just then, my whole face got happy.

"Lucille! Lucille! I just thought of something! You and me can *pretend* we are twins! And we can do everything just the same! And so on Saturday you can come to my house. And I will put nail polish on my nails, just like you! And you will stay home from that birthday party, just like me!"

Lucille didn't say anything back.

I tapped on her.

"How come you're not talking, twin?" I said. "How come you're not saying anything back?"

"'Cause I want to go to the party, that's why," said Lucille.

I did a huffy breath at her.

"Yes, Lucille. I *know* you want to go to the party. But now you and me are twins. And twins have to do everything just the same. And so if *I* don't go to the party, then *you* can't go to the party, too. On account of that is the twin rules."

"No, it's not," said Lucille. "My cousins are twins. And one is a boy. And one is a girl. And they don't do *anything* alike."

I jumped up from my chair.

"Yeah, only that is not the kind of twin I want to be, madam!" I yelled.

Mrs. snapped her loud fingers at me.

"Sit down!" she hollered.

Just then, that Jim I hate turned around in his chair. And he laughed real mean at me. 'Cause I was in trouble.

"Turn around your fatty head!" I said.

Only he didn't turn it around. And so that's how come I had to run to his table. And I had to turn it around for him.

"JUNIE B. JONES!" shouted Mrs. "WHAT ARE YOU DOING?"

"I am turning around his fatty head," I explained.

Mrs. hurried to where I was. Then she quick took my arm. And she marched me into the hall.

She pointed to Principal's office.

"Go!" she said real angry.

I did a gulp.

"Yeah, only I'm not actually supposed to go there anymore," I said. "'Cause me and

Mother had a talk about it. And she said for me not to get sent there again."

Mrs.'s face got red as a tomato.

She started counting numbers.

"One . . . two . . . three . . . four . . ."

And so that's how come I hurried up and walked.

'Cause teachers who count numbers are the scariest kind there is.

7/
My Story This Time
by Junie B. Jones

Principal is the boss of the school.

He lives at the office.

I have to go there when I am unruly.

Unruly is the school word for not being ruly.

There is a typing lady there. She isn't allowed to smile.

"Sit down," she said.

She pointed at the blue chair.

"Yeah, only I don't actually like to sit there, remember that? 'Cause that is where the bad kids sit. And I am not even bad," I explained.

I explain that to her every time I go there.

The typing lady leaned over the counter at me. She made her face look scary at me.

"*Sittttt dowwwwn,*" she said.

I sat down.

Then I pulled my frog jumper over my face. So nobody could see me.

"Pull your skirt back down," said the typing lady.

"Yeah, only I'm actually allowed to do this. 'Cause I have on tights," I said. "See them? They are green with little tadpoles on them."

Just then, I heard Principal's voice.

"Well, well . . . Junie B. Jones. What a surprise," he said.

My mouth dropped all the way opened.

"HEY!" I hollered from under my dress. "HOW DID YOU KNOW IT'S ME UNDER HERE? 'CAUSE YOU CAN'T EVEN SEE MY FACE!"

"Lucky guess," said Principal.

After that, I uncovered my head. And me and him went in his office.

I climbed up in the big wood chair.

Principal looked very tiredish. He rubbed the sides of his baldie head.

"Okay, let's hear it. What's your story this time?" he said.

I sat up straight and tall.

"My Story This Time, by Junie B. Jones.

"Once upon a time, I didn't get invited to a meanie boy's birthday. And I am the *only one* in *all* of Room Nine who isn't going. And so that's how come I was moving today.

Only Mother brought me to school very stiff. And then I was a buzzing bee. Only Crybaby William is a squealer. And Lucille won't be a good twin. And so then Mrs. yelled at me. And that's how come I had to twist that Jim's head. And now I am sitting here in this big wood chair."

I folded my hands on my lap.

"The end."

Principal put his head down on his desk.

I peeked at him.

"Are you laying low?" I whispered.

He sat up again. Then he called my mother on the telephone.

Those two talk very often.

This time, they talked about the birthday party. And how I'm not invited.

After he hanged up, Principal looked nicer at me.

"I guess sometimes we grown-ups think we're the only ones with problems," he said. "We forget that even when you're little, life can be tough. Can't it, Junie B. Jones?"

"Yes," I said. "Life can get your goat."

After that, me and him went out of his office. And he lifted me into the blue chair again.

"I want you to wait here a minute," he said. "There's someone I have to talk to before I can get this settled."

"Yeah, only guess what? I don't actually want to sit in this chair," I explained. "On account of this is where the bad kids sit. And I'm not even bad."

Principal thought and thought. Then he snapped his fingers.

"I think I might have the perfect solution," he said.

He went in his office and brought out a giant shopping bag.

"What if we hide you under here?" he asked. "If we hide you under this bag, no one will be able to see you at all."

I jumped up and down very excited. 'Cause hiding is my favorite thing in the whole world, that's why!

Principal sat me down in the chair.

He put that giant shopping bag over my head.

"HEY! WHO TURNED OUT THE LIGHTS?" I said.

Then I laughed and laughed. 'Cause that is called *comedy*, of course.

I bended my knees and pulled them under the bag. I hugged them real tight.

"Now all you can see is the tippy-toes of my shoes!" I said very happy.

"This is the perfectest solution I ever saw! And so how did you even think of this wonderful thing?" I asked.

Only Principal didn't answer me back.

'Cause he probably went back to his office already.

After that I hided and hided inside my bag.

I hided a real long time.

It was a jillion years, I think.

"Guess what? This is taking longer than a minute," I said from inside there.

The typing lady didn't answer me.

"Yeah, only guess what else? My knees are very bended and squished in here," I said. "And so this isn't good for my circle-lation, probably."

Just then, my legs started squirming all around. 'Cause I was getting ants in my pants, that's why!

"HEY! DOESN'T ANYBODY HAVE EARS? GET ME OUTTA HERE RIGHT NOW! 'CAUSE I AM AT THE END OF

MY ROPE IN THIS THING! PLUS ALSO,
I AM GETTING ANTS IN MY . . ."

All of a sudden, someone yanked the
bag right off my head.

It was the scary typing lady.

". . . pants," I said very soft.

She took me back into Principal's office.

And guess what?

That Jim was in there!

He was sitting in the big wood chair!

And Principal was frowning at him!

"Junie B., our friend Jim here has something he wants to say to you. Don't you,
Jim?" asked Principal.

That meanie Jim didn't answer. He kept
on looking at his feet.

Principal tapped his fingers.

"We're *waiting*, Jim," he said.

Then that Jim did a huffy breath. And

he said the words *I'm sorry.*

Principal raised up his eyebrows.

"Sorry for what, Jim? Tell Junie B. what you're sorry for."

That Jim stared at his feet some more.

"I'm sorry I didn't give her an invitation to my party," he said very grumpity.

"But your mother *told* you to, didn't she, Jim?" said Principal. "Your mother told you to give an invitation to every single person in your class. But you got mad at Junie B. And you decided not to give her one. Isn't that right?"

That meanie boy did his shoulders up and down.

"I guess," he said real soft.

Principal crossed his arms.

"And so what are you going to do to correct the problem?" he asked.

That Jim waited and waited.

Then—all of a sudden—he got down from his chair.

And he holded out an invitation to me.

My stomach did a flippy flop.

"For me? Is that really for me!" I said very squealing.

Then I snatched that thing right out of his hand. And I zoomed all around the room.

"Oh boy!" I said. "It's really for me! It's really for me! And so now I'm not the *only one*!"

I zoomed all around the big wood chair.

Principal looked nervous of me.

He hurried up and opened his door.

Then I zoomed right out of there!

And I didn't stop till I got to Room Nine!

8/
Ruining My Saturday

On Saturday, Mother woke me up from sleeping.

"We have to go to the store and buy Jim a present," she said.

I did a sleepy yawn.

"Yeah, only I don't actually like that boy," I explained. "And so you can go by yourself. And I will trust your judgment."

I pulled the covers over my head.

Mother pulled them off again.

Then she made me get dressed.

And she made me eat a banana.

And she made me go to the store with her.

She holded my hand and pulled me behind her.

"Since we don't know what he already has, let's get him something unusual," she said.

"Let's get him greasy, grimy gopher guts. That is unusual," I said.

Mother made a sick face.

She pulled me through the store.

We went past the bathroom stuff.

I pointed.

"*That*. Let's get him *that*," I said. "*That* is unusual."

Mother sucked in her cheeks.

"We're not getting him a toilet brush," she said.

She pulled me past the pet stuff.

"*That.* Let's get him *that,*" I said. "*That* is unusual."

But Mother said, "No choke chain."

Just then, she pulled me past the tools.

That's when my eyes popped right out of my head!

"THAT! LET'S GET HIM THAT! LOOK, MOTHER! LOOK! I LOVE THAT THING!"

I runned to it speedy quick.

"IT'S A TOOL BELT! SEE? IT'S JUST LIKE GRAMPA MILLER'S! ONLY IT'S MADE FOR LITTLE CHILDREN LIKE ME! SEE IT, MOTHER? SEE THIS WONDERFUL THING!"

Mother took it down off the shelf.

"Look!" I said. "It has a hammer! And a screwdriver! And some pliers! And a flashlight! And a real actual level with a bubble in it! Plus also, there's a pocket with little pretend nails in the front."

I jumped all around.

"Can I try it on? Can I? Please, Mother? Please? Please?"

Mother shook her head no.

"We're not shopping for you today, Junie B. We're shopping for Jim, remember?"

"I know it. I know we are shopping for that Jim," I said. "And so this can be for his birthday. Only first I have to try it on to see if it fits. 'Cause him and me are both the same size, I bet!"

Finally, Mother fastened the tool belt on me.

"Ooooh! It has Velcro!" I said. "I love this stickery stuff! Can we buy it? Please, Mother? Can we buy it? And take it home to my house?"

Mother thought and thought.

"I don't know, Junie B. Something tells me this isn't a good idea. I'm afraid you'll want to keep it."

"No, I won't! I won't want to keep it. I promise, Mother! I promise! I promise!"

And so finally Mother gave in to me. And she bought the wonderful tool belt.

I held it on my lap all the way home in the car.

Then I runned into the house. And I zoomed to my room. And I put that thing on me again.

"Now I can do odd jobs!" I said real thrilled.

I took the hammer and tapped on my wall.

Then I screwed a screw with the screw-driver.

Plus also, I twisted my Teddy's nose off
with the pliers. Only I actually didn't mean
to do that one.

I patted his head.

"Breathe through your mouth," I said.

Just then, Mother's voice hollered to me.

"JUNIE B.! IT'S TIME TO TAKE YOUR BATH, HONEY!"

I did a frown. 'Cause Mother was a little mixed up, I think.

I hollered back.

"YEAH, ONLY I DON'T EVEN HAVE TO TAKE A BATH TODAY! ON ACCOUNT OF TODAY IS SATURDAY! AND SATURDAY IS MY DIRTY DAY!"

Mother came in my room.

"I *know* today is Saturday, Junie B.," she said. "But you're going to a birthday party. And when you go to a birthday party, you have to take a bath. Plus we're going to have to wash and curl your hair."

I backed up from her.

"No," I said. "'Cause nobody even

explained that to me before. And so that doesn't even make sense. On account of I hate that meanie kid. So how come I have to get clean for him?"

Mother looked at the end of her rope.

"When you go to a party, you take a bath. Period. End of discussion," she said.

Then she left my room. And she went to start the tub.

I sat on my bed very glum.

"Darn it," I said. "'Cause that stupid boy is ruining my whole entire Saturday."

Mother hollered some more.

"JUNIE B.? COULD YOU BRING ME THE TOOL BELT, PLEASE? I NEED TO GET IT WRAPPED!"

"Darn it," I said again.

'Cause I didn't even want to give that to him.

I looked down at it.

I touched all the wonderful tools.

"I love this darned thing," I said real sad.

"I'M WAITING!" shouted Mother.

But I still didn't take it to her.

Just then, I heard the bath water turn off.

My heart got very pumpy.

"Oh no!" I said. "'Cause now she's gonna come get me! And she will take my tool belt away! And she will wrap it up for that meanie guy!"

I jumped off my bed and runned around my room.

"I gotta hide! I gotta hide!"

I runned all over everywhere.

"Darn it! 'Cause there's not even a good hiding place in this dumb room!" I said.

"JUNIE B.!" Mother screamed.

I heard her feet!

They were coming for me, I think!

"Oh no!" I said. "Oh no! Oh no!"

Then all of a sudden, I quick grabbed my wonderful tool belt!

And I zoomed to my door!

And I tried to nail that thing shut with my hammer!

9/

The Only One
in Room Nine

Mother runned into my room.

'Cause pretend nails don't actually work, apparently.

"JUNIE B. JONES! WHAT IN THE WORLD ARE YOU DOING IN HERE?" she shouted.

She looked at my door.

Her eyes got very bulging.

"YOU WERE *HAMMERING?*" she yelled. "YOU WERE TRYING TO HAMMER *NAILS???* . . . IN YOUR *DOOR?*"

Just then, Daddy runned in, too.

"WHERE IN THE WORLD DID YOU GET A HAMMER?" he yelled.

"Tell him, Junie B.! Tell your father where you got the hammer!" growled Mother.

I pointed at her.

"*She* gave it to me," I said.

Just then, steam came out of Mother's head.

"NO! I DID *NOT* GIVE YOU THAT HAMMER, JUNIE B.! THAT HAMMER WAS FOR JIM! AND YOU KNOW IT!"

After that, Mother picked me up. And she sat me on my bed. And she growled more mad words at me.

They were . . . I cannot be trusted to have a real actual hammer. And I cannot be trusted to have a real actual tool belt. And I am never, ever allowed to have nails until I am all grown up and I live in my own apartment.

Daddy walked up and down in front of me.

"Why, Junie B.? Why would you do such a thing? Why would you ever try to nail your door shut?" he said.

I started to cry a little bit.

"Because," I said.

"Because *why*?" he grouched.

"Because I felt pressure inside me," I said. "Because that party is ruining my whole entire Saturday. Because first I had to shop. And then Mother said I had to get a bath and wash my hair. Only I don't even *like* that meanie head boy. And so how come I have to get clean and give him that wonderful tool belt? 'Cause what kind of deal is that?"

Mother did an angry breath.

"This was *your* decision, Junie B.," she said. "*You're* the one who wanted to go to the party. No one is making you do it."

I wiped my nose on my sweater sleeve.

"Yeah, only if I don't go, I will be the *only one* in Room Nine," I said. "And that is the saddest story I ever heard of."

Daddy sat down next to me.

"Why?" he said. "Why is it sad to spend your Saturday the way *you* want to spend it? Why is it sad to spend the day having *fun,* instead of wasting it on a boy you don't like?"

Mother sat down, too.

"That doesn't sound sad to me," said Mother. "That sounds *good,* in fact."

"No, that does *not* sound good," I said very snapping. "What is so good about being the *only one*?"

Daddy did his shoulders up and down.

"Lots of things," he said. "Like you'll be the *only one* who doesn't have to take a bath. Have you ever thought of that?"

"And you'll be the *only one* who doesn't have to wash her hair," said Mother.

"*And,*" said Daddy, "you'll be the *only one* in Room Nine who doesn't have to give Jim a present. How 'bout *that* one? Huh?"

I sat up a little bit straighter.

'Cause *that* one was excellent, that's why.

Mother ruffled my hair.

"And what about Grampa Miller?" she asked. "You haven't forgotten that he invited you to his house today, have you?"

Just then, my whole mouth came open.

'Cause I *did* forget about that!

"The toilet!" I said. "I forgot about the

toilet! 'Cause me and Grampa were going to fix that thing! And we were going to touch that big ball that floats on top!"

Mother made a face.

"Lovely," she said.

"I *know* it is lovely," I said. "And so I have to get over there right now. Or else Grandma is gonna get to touch it, and not me."

Then Mother looked at me very strange.

And Daddy went to get his keys.

Mother and Daddy made me take the tool belt back to the store.

They made me give it to the man.

"Here," I said. "I cannot be trusted with this wonderful thing."

The man smiled kind of sad.

"Sorry, sis," he said.

"That's okay," I said. "'Cause the nails didn't actually work that good."

He gave me my money back.

"Maybe when you're older," he said.

"Maybe," I said. "Plus also, I might get a toilet brush."

After the store, I went to my grampa Miller's.

He was working in his garden.

I ran my fastest at him.

"GRAMPA MILLER! HEY, GRAMPA MILLER! DID YOU FIX IT YET? DID YOU ALREADY FIX THE TOILET?"

He twirled me around.

"Not yet!" he said. "Not yet I didn't! I've been waitin' for you!"

And so just then, me and him hurried up.

And we got our tools.
And we runned upstairs.
Then we took the lid right off that thing!
And I flushed all the water right out of it!

I touched the big ball!

"This is fun! Right, Grampa? Right? This is the time of our life!" I said.

"Sure it is! Of course it is!" said my grampa Frank Miller.

I laughed very happy.

"Hey, Grampa. Guess what? I am the *only one*!" I said.

He looked confused at me.

"I am the *only one* in Room Nine who is fixin' a toilet!" I explained.

Then Grampa Miller laughed, too. "You're really somethin'," he said.

"You're really somethin', too, Grampa," I said back.

Then I hugged him real tight.

And I climbed up on his lap.

And I told him a secret in his ear.

"And guess what else?" I whispered. "I still would like a goat."

Love laughing with Junie B. Jones?

Then join the

today
at
JunieBKidsClub.com

GAMES! JOKES! PHOTOS!
A SCRAPBOOK!

RHCB

Illustrations © 2013 by Denise Brunkus, from the Junie B. Jones® series, by Barbara Park.

Hello, school children! Hello! Hello! It's me . . . Junie B., First Grader!

I have been going to school for over one and a half entire years now. And I have learned a jillion things that will help you survive at that place.

And guess what?

NOW I AM GOING TO PASS THIS INFORMATION ON TO Y-O-U!!!

I wrote it all down in my brand-new book!

It is called: Junie B.'s Essential Survival Guide to School!

All of the tips and drawings are done by me, Junie B. Jones!

Plus also, there are stickers and pages for you to write in!

This thing is a hoot, I tell you!

Don't miss these other great books by Barbara Park!

Rah! Rah! Rah!
Join the crowd.
Read these books
And laugh out loud!

Junie B. has a lot to say about
everything and everybody in
Barbara Park's Junie B. Jones books!

the baby's room

Mother and Daddy fixed up a room for the new baby.
It's called a nursery. Except I don't know why. Because
a baby isn't a nurse, of course.

• from *Junie B. Jones and a Little Monkey Business*

school words

After that, the mop got removed from us. *Removed* is
the school word for snatched right out of our hands.

• from *Junie B. Jones and Her Big Fat Mouth*

rules

Me and Mother had a little talk. It was called—*no
screaming back off, clown.* Only I never even heard of
that rule before.

• from *Junie B. Jones and the Yucky Blucky Fruitcake*

her baby brother

His name is Ollie. I love him a real lot. Except I wish
he didn't live at my actual house.

• from *Junie B. Jones and That Meanie Jim's Birthday*